This Storybook Belongs To

Princess _____

A Moment to Remember

ADVANCE PUBLISHERS

Princess Aurora sighed. She loved Prince Phillip, but life in the palace was so very different. Tonight there would be yet another royal ball, and her guardian fairies were bickering over what she should wear.

Aurora looked out the window. She missed the quiet of the glade where she had met Phillip.

"Now, dears," said Flora, "let's not argue. We all know that this outfit suits Aurora best. Don't you think so, Aurora?"

Before Aurora could answer, the royal chef entered the room to ask the princess's approval of an ice sculpture.

At last Prince Phillip came into the room.

"Hello, dearest," he said.

"Oh, Phillip, I'm so glad to see you. I—" Aurora began.

"A-hem." The royal florist interrupted. "Princess Aurora, could you please tell the royal table setter that she must place flowers in the middle of each table tonight?"

"Princess Aurora," said the royal table setter, "could you please tell the royal florist that our guests will never see one another if I put his big flower arrangements in the middle of each table?"

"Why don't you just put a single flower on each table?" said Aurora.

The two servants looked at her, horrified. "A single flower?" they muttered as they left. "The guests will be so insulted!"

"You were saying, dear?" Phillip asked.

"Pardon me, Princess Aurora." The Royal Steward bowed deeply. "But I must have your approval on the seating arrangements."

"Thank you, Steward," said Princess Aurora. "I will look at them—"

"As soon as we return," Prince Phillip finished.

Both Aurora and the Steward looked at Phillip in surprise.

"Where are we going, Phillip?" Aurora asked.

Phillip smiled. "Out for a ride where no one can ask us anything."

As they mounted their horses, Phillip turned to Aurora. "I'm sorry, dearest. I had forgotten that the Royal Equestrian Guard must come with us."

Aurora looked at the ten riders behind them and tried to hide her disappointment. Then she leaned down and whispered to Phillip's horse. Whinnying, Samson charged away from the palace with Phillip. Aurora's horse, Mirette, dashed after them, leaving the Royal Guard far behind.

"Whooaa! Whoa, Samson!" Phillip shouted as Samson raced ahead.

"It's all right, Phillip," Aurora called.

They galloped into the forest, where Samson found a path through the trees. Then he left the path and stopped suddenly.

SPLASH! Phillip sailed over Samson's head and landed in a stream.

"No carrots for you, boy!" Prince Phillip scolded his horse. He looked up and saw Aurora trying to hide a smile.

"Do you remember this place, Phillip?" Aurora asked.

Phillip sloshed out of the stream. He pulled off his boots and dumped the water out of them.

Aurora took off her shoes, too. She spun around gracefully, humming a tune. "Yes," Prince Phillip said softly. "I remember this place…."

"I will never forget that day," said Aurora, "no matter how crowded our lives become with royal visitors and royal duties."

Prince Phillip smiled and touched her face. "Nor will I. For when I am with you, all others disappear."

Phillip and Aurora smiled, wishing they could bring the peace and love they had known in the glade back to the palace.

Their peaceful moment ended as the Royal Equestrians thundered into the glade.

Phillip put on his boots and cape. Then he picked up a fallen flower and handed it to Aurora.

Aurora took the gift and smiled. "We should go back to get ready for tonight," she said.

"You go ahead, dear," Phillip said. "I'll be back soon."

Aurora nodded and smiled. Yes, that would give her plan a head start.

Meanwhile, Phillip had a plan of his own.

"Not a word of this to the princess," he said to her animal friends as he gathered some flowers.

For the rest of the afternoon, Princess Aurora worked on Phillip's surprise. Servants moved tables, laid tablecloths, and gathered flowers. Flora, Fauna, and Merryweather flitted about, helping wherever they could.

More than once, Aurora heard a servant murmur, "Our guests will certainly be...surprised."

Aurora just smiled. "It is Prince Phillip I want to surprise," she said. "Not a word of this to him."

That night, Flora, Fauna, and Merryweather had just helped Aurora dress in the gown of her choice when Prince Phillip came into the room. He held out a simple crown he had made from flowers. "Would you like to wear this, too?" he asked.

"Oh, Phillip!" Aurora put on the flower crown and hugged her husband. "It is perfect for this evening."

"Now, I have a surprise for you!" Aurora led Phillip down the stairs to the ballroom. It was dark and empty.

"You've canceled the ball?" Prince Phillip asked. "Have the guests left?"

"No, Phillip." Aurora touched her flower crown. "You brought our little glade back to me. Now let me take you back to our little glade."

In the courtyard, a sweet breeze whispered through the flowers and trees. Water danced in the fountain. Candles flickered in the darkness like the stars above them.

"The glade will always be in our hearts," Aurora whispered. "But now it is in our palace, too."

Prince Phillip whispered in reply, "Then we should dance."

Just then Phillip's father, King Hubert, approached.

"This is much better than the stuffy balls I usually attend," he said to Princess Aurora. "Thank you, my dear!"

And as Aurora and Phillip danced,
their little friends added their own
magic from the glade.